For My Cousin Judy

Houghton Mifflin/Clarion Books
52 Vanderbilt Avenue, New York, NY 10017

Copyright © 1981 by Dick Gackenbach

Library of Congress Cataloging in Publication Data
Gackenbach, Dick.   Little bug.
SUMMARY: His fears keep a little bug in his dark and dreary hole until a
mysterious voice convinces him that the beauties of the world are worth a
few risks.
[1. Insects—Fiction]   I. Title.
PZ7.G117Li   [E]   80-21213
ISBN: 0-395-30080-0

LITTLE BUG

BY DICK GACKENBACH

 Houghton Mifflin/Clarion Books/New York

"LITTLE BUG!" a loud Voice thundered.
"WHY ARE YOU HIDING IN
   THAT DARK AND DREARY HOLE?"

"Because I'm very tiny," said the Bug.

"SO?" the Voice said.

"If I leave this hole," said the Bug,
"a bird might peck at me."

"IT MIGHT!" the Voice agreed.

"Or," said the Bug, "I might be flattened by a big and heavy sneaker."

"ALAS," said the Voice,
"THAT, TOO, COULD COME TO PASS!"

"Or I might end up inside a jelly jar,"
said the Bug. "And starve to death!"

"THAT IS TRUE, LITTLE BUG,"
said the Voice. "VERY TRUE."

"So why should I leave my
nice safe hole?" asked the Bug.

"TO TRAVEL ON THE WIND," said the Voice.

"AND FEEL THE WARMTH OF THE SUN."

"AND TO TASTE THE SWEET NECTAR OF THE ROSE, MY LITTLE BUG!"

Then the Voice spoke no more.

And so the little Bug
decided to leave the safety
of his dark hole.

He was carried on the soft winds,
and he skimmed across the cool waters.

He played among the earthy grasses,
and ate from the tasty flower.
He was a very happy little Bug.

In time,
he met another Bug.
"I love you!" he said.
"And I love you,"
the other Bug told him.

Together they built a fine nest
inside a piece of wood
and soon many little Bugs
were born.

One day, the Voice
spoke to the Bug again.

"LITTLE BUG!" the Voice said.
"DO THE BIRDS
STILL PECK AT YOU?"

"Oh yes," said the Bug.
"All the time!"

"WHAT ABOUT THE SNEAKERS?"
the Voice asked.
"DO THEY STILL
TRY TO FLATTEN YOU?"

"Yes they do," said the Bug.

"AND ARE YOU STILL IN DANGER
OF BEING TRAPPED
INSIDE A JELLY JAR?"

"Very often," answered the Bug.

"WELL THEN," said the Voice,
"WOULDN'T YOU RATHER
RETURN TO YOUR DARK AND
DREARY HOLE WHERE IT'S SAFE?"

"No!" said the Bug. "Never!"

"GOOD FOR YOU," said the Voice.
"YOU ARE TRULY FULL OF SPUNK.
 CARRY ON, LITTLE BUG! CARRY ON!"

And the voice spoke no more.